Moments That Carry:
Through the eyes of Peter

By

Petar Kostadinov

Published by Petar Kostadinov

Through www.pajkpublishing.com

FIRST PRINTING

U.S.A

Cover Design by Petar Kostadinov © 2014

This book is fiction. Any resemblance, to places, people, events, is purely coincidental.
ISBN-13: 978-0692355602 (pajkpublishing)

ISBN-10: 069235560X

Moments That Carry by Petar Kostadinov ©2014

CONTENTS

Prologue

Many years ago the planet endured hardships. It flew from one

side to the
next as the sun
revolved
around it.
Behind that
dreary
moment one
day the meteor
flew by and
struck it with
impeccable

force.

Everything on it just scrambled to find a place to hide. Those that survived had a chance to live on within the Grace of God.

Those that did not, had been forced by nature to go up in Heaven on the higher ground.

When time first was created, it was not to keep it

in track. It was however to know where everyone was going. The idea was that, each of us, humans or not, have longed to belong to the road ahead.

And even
though the
peace of mind
had a
dilligance it
surely
unturned its
road that once
had been
unbroken.
So, it seems

that every piece of land belonged to everyone. The human beings had been born and they created something of a melting pot. It was the story

of human
nature. We
were here to
learn, live,
sing, cherish
everything
that was
sustained and
given to us by
the Grace Of
God.

Some days they fought and claimed what was theirs. Brothers against brothers, sisters against sisters, fought for land and separation of each other. With naming each country and land, it became of a new world. So many times had it been just sliced. It was as if,

GOD had been now crying and he could not believe what he had been seeing.

To the eyes of Heroes and to the eyes of those that foresaw that

the rain was
going to fall
upon and
change the
hearts of the
human heart.

I was There

I could be wrong. But I know that the road was mine to take. Each fiddle of songs, each dreary

moment was
scars. Then
again, it was
mine to
sustain. I
walked for
miles and
miles till the
sunrise arose
and the sunset
went down.

I could not
drink or think.
I was just kin
to know why I
was here, and
may I not
know how
much the river
flowed to be
winded down,
in those

promises.
   "Take care"
he said to me
   'I will. I am
going to keep
this fiddle
with me and
play it when I
need to live' I
told him with
my shy voice

As the day drowned, I found myself in the new city around 3am pacific time. I could not believe my eyes. There was something in the distance.

But even if it
was not, what
I thought it
could be, I
realized that
each day had
its songs
purified with
morningfull
light.
   The frowned

face of an old
man. If it were
not for him,
we were not
going to be
here. His
blood flowed
in us. Died on
a cross,
became the
Fundamental

Light to the
human race.
His Kindness
was us.

Somehow I
knew that for
that dreary
moment I
stood there
and he spoke

to me, while
he was leaving
us and yet he
was not.
"Once, I go,
you will take
over my
teachings.
Never fear the
ones that do
not like you.

One day, they will realize how important you are. To them you are Rock" As he spoke to me, I knew what he meant. But only GOD himself would

say it. And yes,
he was one.

'I will let the
world know of
you' I spoke to
him

"I know. I
will also come
back to you
and all of
them when

everyone is
much more
wiser and that
in written
stone you will
read for the
ages of time"
He spoke to
me wisely
   I never
forgot that

moment. He did choose me and I was his number one. My name spoke of it all. But in a sense, now I had the obligation to contain this world as he had.

I also believe
even though
his body is
gone, his spirit
watches me
every day;
what I do, and
who I help
out.

When
I Have to

Days became
night. I was
about to fall
asleep. I did
not have a

tired heart in me. I kept on going. I had to, for I was given a Job of a Lifetime. The future depended on me.

Even though it had been

late, I called
upon Paul.
Here we did
not have any
phones. I send
a messenger
with a written
sheet letter,
made out of
the sheep's
coat.

I wanted to discuss how important it was for us to keep Jesus's legacy alive. By now, John was gone and it was us two. Matthew just wanted to be

private and
even though
he came by to
speak with us
he still was
devoting his
life after life
of Jesus.

I was
amazed that
the steps we

took, to get
here. It burned
us all inside.
Yet, we know,
we shall see
them again.
   From this
point onward.
The road was
tough. You can
imagine how

many miles
we had to go.
Paul and I just
looked at each
other and saw
the sea coming
up in front of
our eyes that
God had given
us.
  I never

understood nature. But was the fisherman OF man. I love nature. But to know it, I was just not so sure where to begin with. Yet I studied it.

Each day was a new beginning. We had to stop at this sea to have some water. Our bodies and minds were dry. God gave us that and we need it to survive. Our journey was long. Many of the town's people were happy that we were there to reach out to them in hope. Jesus left us

with words of
wisdom. I saw
in many of
people's eyes,
that they need
it help. Hope
that to be
endured for
life time.

But the wars
that are fought

and were
fought then,
were all about
the teachings
that God
himself had
written. Those
good words.
That for some
nonbelievers
were on the

side of the Evil. The world needs peace. Primarily in the days of Revelation. Humans were created by the image of God himself.

Even though
each and
everyone has a
different voice,
style of
walking, being
who they are.
We are all the
same inside
our hearts.
Just great

human beings.
For now, the
bread we eat is
Gods temple,
and the water
we drink is his
pure light. The
red wine he
created from
Grapes, is his
heart. But

never the less,
you are true
you and the
road that you
must take is
goodness. Stay
away from
Evil. God
makes it clear.

That Good
Prevails over
Evil. Good
always wins.

Those Dreams You Need

Like Jesus,
so can you.
Follow the
road that you

have taken to create. To bring out of you. If you want that farm to raise Goat, vegetables, Cows, Chicken's...go ahead. Because

people need to
be fed and
they need to
eat. You are
Gods greatest
miracle. You
provide them
with energy.
If you are
going to write
the next best

novel. Take leaf from the tree and start writing. The Bible was written on a sheep's skin. And it was best to realize that every page turned great.

Later that evening Paul and I met up with Matthew. He was sitting in his temple and reading the great words God had given him.

In part that we ate, we remembered what Jesus did for us. He was our savior and most of all our brother. I know he chose us to be his apostle. We

had been
separated for
years.

By the time
the Roman
army found all
of us as we
were
preaching
Gods Good
word, we were

in hiding. All of us had families. Jesus had one too. But it was never revealed to the public, because he was one and only Son Of God.

We knew. He left legacy. Mary 2 was his wife. The one he left behind. Yes, it was the same name as his mother's. And the Mary

which was one
of the
Apostles.
 He had a son
and daughter.
As I had two
son's and so
did Paul and
Matthew, and
John, James,
and the rest of

us.

But we had
to follow him.
He chose us.
As he had
been chosen
by God.

As we
walked now
for miles again,
we had to

preach separately. Paul decided to head out to Town Near Greece. I have decided to go in Greece and by this time, I reached the spoken word

from God to
the people
there.

Matthew
went back
East. He
preached
peace there as
well. Among
the natural
way that God

told us to care
for each other.
Never forget
the light that
shines from
above is the
Star miracle
that we need
to keep it
sacred.

When I Left The Storm

By now I
was pieces
away
from the front
door or the
heart that

Just spoke to me as I frolicked around Gods Temple. He had built one for me with heavy steady stones. The House Of God as it was called. Everyone came and prayed here. The morning after. When Jesus showed up, speaking to me, to still believe. That all the right

things I did,
and thought
that were not
as best as I
have thought
to believe.
I headed on
the Northern
Side of the
planet. There I
met with

Thomas. Who was the one that let his heart preach the very best of Jesus and God. The word of love was intrust upon him. We shared the

knowledge
and decided to
meet up again
in 9 months
along with
Paul, to head
over to Rome.
  It was then
when we
started to fill
the grounds

with stones, where our church would be build. God chose that side for a reason. It was the center of the Universe. People would gather there

and they will
pray for
greatness and
forgiveness
from the
Almighty.
The water
fountain was
where God
asked his first
son to come,

built and drink
from it. From
that moment
on, life began
purity.

Not a day
went by of
which we rose
to bring hope,
peace to each

animal, human
on the first
living planet
of the sun and
the moon.

The Incredible Road

When the day came for I to go upon on my own and

take the word
to them, was
when God
appointed me
as his number
one. He did
build the
church for me.
He trusted my
heart, my
judgment, that

I was the one that will preach the great light.

It began in the early 40AD. I was old enough to know much about life now. But as I was

fishing and out
of calmness
and frustration
that I could
not catch
anything that
day. This
stranger with
longer hair
than mine,
with big smile

approached me and said "I see you need some help. I will help you"

'No thanks. I don't need any help. It is just too damn hard to fetch anything to eat today' I told him

"Peter, I will help you. Let me do what God himself had given me. You know, people await your blessings"

And with
that magic
heart.He
reached in the
waters with
his hand, and
in one moment,
fish gathered.
They swarmed
in the net.
Astonishing.

"But, How?" I asked
"If you believe, all the great things are possible."
He was the chosen one. After this moment, came the time when

he said to me
"Come with
me Peter. Join
me. Let's heal
the World
together."
'But, why? I
am no good. I
can't do magic.
I am just a
simple

fisherman.'
  "Come, I
will make you
fisherman of
Man"
  And I
followed him.
I had doubts
on my mind.
Who was still
this man. But I

knew down in my heart that he was the chosen one. The one everyone will call King. Simple word. Yet, he told us, not to call him that. Because

he was just
like us.
Though he
was chosen
one for the
people, to lead
them into
salvation.
   He died on a
cross to save
our lives. He

told many
stories. He
helped a man
see again. He
healed a man
that could not
hear. He
awoke a child
from death. As
well his cousin
Lazaros.

Many that
did not believe,
later on started
to wonder.
Jesus, also
healed man's
cut out ear.
But why was
he able to do
that? How was

he able to do that magic?

Later in the centuries there will be Doctors. That will do such miracles. For those that they can help.

See, Jesus

was not
perfect always.
He healed
those that
needed more
time on Earth.
Those that
were ready,
like God said,
were to join
them with him

up in Heaven.
He gives out
wings upon
arrival. God
has ranks like
on Earth. So,
those that have
higher points
while being
here on Earth
and done some

superior jobs, they are awarded Golden wings. Those that are less than that one rank lower are silver and bronze. But they play significant role on Earth from Heaven.

The one big example and the one same role they all play is that they all protect from harm and evil.

Each person,

and animal, has a guardian angel hanging around them. Some have more than one or two.

It could be their loved ones that have passed on.

Even though I was also chosen by Jesus, I have my long lost family protecting me. I know this by fact.

Because the spiritual world is aways among us

There have Been Moments

Like I always knew. But If I did deny him 3 times, did not

mean I did not care or loved him. He knew that I had to do it. He was protecting my life. Because was sacrificing his for all of us and humanity.

I believe
that everyone
denies
someone else.
Not because
they do not
believe,
because
some times
someone has
told them,

like example, "Your children are not yours" Mother to a Father.

But Eve never done that. Maybe it all comes to being the

new Single
Parent, and
the Law that
was written.
Money given
to those they
claim such a
thing.
Without
asking for
acknowledg

ment of the other involved party. To sign or not to sign the paper.

So here we have the same similar situation. I

cared for
Jesus. And
still do.
I never
denied my
kids. She
denied us,
and never
asked me.
But The
Lord, also

asked me not to give up. To care for them and to love them. To forgive them. If they have done me wrong. It was never my children's

fault. But
their mother
who I
forgave by
Gods will to
let it go and
be his temple
upon which
he will build
his Home.

The Road That Promised

One of those days, as we have called upon James to join

us on this
trip, he who
was believer
in the Higher
Light. He
who proven
that his
majesty
exists.

But He
never taken

that same
longer roads
as we others
did. Never
was he
chosen to
lead as much
as us.

He wrote
some letters
from God to

the people.
Added the
verses of
light and
continued to
live secluded
life.
   We
unwillingly
took the road
and justified

the days we
were
changing the
people for
good.
   I remember
the stories
taken from
Jesus to God
and then us.
How Moses,

took to the
Mountain
and God
Almighty
gave him the
written
words that
were to be
sown in the
hearts of the
people of the

planet Earth. From the beginning of time. God could have simply given the ten commandme nts to Adam and Eve. But he had to

wait till he
came along
to chose him
and
afterwards
the fact of
knowledge
began.

From The moment On

The tear in
my eyes,
were so
much as

though I
could not
bear the pain
inside my
heart. I was
right, for
taking the
path as God
has asked me
to do so. The
words of

heroism that
for every
step I had
done, was
just alright.
Matthew
wrote me a
letter. We
knew that we
were going
to go like

Jesus. Each
of us knew.
But God
himself was
with us.
　　We spoke
of truth. We
spoke of
hope. We
spoke of love.
Love

between
humanity.
Peace that
must reside
among each
of us.
   In
meantime as
we walked
the road that
lead us to

brand new
years, we
discovered
the
possibility
that not one
bit of what
we do is
impossible.
The spoken
good word

always prevailed. It was such a incredible journey. The morning after we slept, prayed, ate. We went to the town's people to discuss more about the gracious Lord.

We met up with James at this point. He had been teaching the people in town of

nearby
Jerusalem.
He ended
up going to
Ireland to
spread a
good word.
With success
he devised a
role. To
leave them a

book of which he had written.

By now, everyone had it in their hands. The bible studies were remarkable. So, we asked

him, if he
could join us
once more to
travel the
World
together. To
give out
hope and
unmistakable
power of the
light that was

shined upon
us from
Jesus.

So, we
headed to the
Eastern Star.
Then went to
the Southern
and
journeyed
across the

seven seas.
The Almighty Jordan River was just as magnificent as ever. The species that

God created,
was an
amazing out
tranquility.

It was Back Then

As the road
came to be
beautiful.
The Lord

showed us
the way. It
had to be
there. When
we went to
see the light,
it was just as
matter of
time.

Here we were, step closer to when we began walking. Thomas, was so concerned that we would not be able to reach

the sunken
ship.
 "We will
not get there.
The storms
are heavy.
The sun is
burning my
eyes, my
heart, my
soul, my

mind."
'Yes, and
that is why
we have to
make it.
Even though
every path
we
Took, we
must realize
that was for

the better of
the people.
This great
Nation.
  Sometimes
storms are not
easy to
conquer.

God Endours All

It had been his flock from the moment he created Adam and Eve. From

the moment he
set foot on the
ground to
paint this
magical
universe. As
wide as wiser.
He knew that
problems
would arise.
But he knew

also, that those
things will be
workout
among every
one.
   This planet
and other ones
like us have
many religions.
For most part
God had many

sons and
daughters. For
greatness he
sent them over.
To be peaceful
amongst one
another.

God loves
each one of
his flock. He
sent many

foods. Many different music. Because without it, this world would not have been possible.

His greatest song upon which he let

unspoken was
that in time
when he sends
Jesus back, to
rescue the rest,
for then this
planet as they
spoke would
be reborn
again.
    If Man

behaves as
such in great
ness. Then all
will be alright.
Miracles are
unbroken.
Dreams that
some one has
shown to have
success had
been risen

from the none
hope believers
to stand up for
the man next
to it.

To know more About the author visit

http://www.amazon.com/Petar-K
ostadinov/e/B00IRJKJHK/ref=sr
_tc_2_0?qid=1419139991&sr=1-
2-ent

www.pajkpublishing.com

https://www.youtube.com/channe
l/UCzuQvvoie-FbA_xftNYBS3g

Notes

<u>Notes</u>